Sherlock Holmes

URBAN FANTASY MYSTERIES 3

John Pirillo

CULT OF THE BLOOD ORCHID

Dark Shadows Surface

CHANDNI CHOWK MARKETPLACE
Old Delhi, India
Now

Gandhi wiped at the sweat on his brow. The city was sweltering with heat and humidity from the monsoons that had been striking. Several dozen of its citizens, the older and the noticeably young had died from the heat and the humidity.

It was sad, but in a country where millions more were even worse off, it was hard to carry guilt for one's own good fortune or misery of another's loss for long. He had a mission to complete now; it gave him purpose. And purpose was what he needed more than anything else.

He stopped at a shop where fresh chapattis were being baked on an open slab of clay heated from below by a fire, pumped by a foot driven bellows.

He felt a slight softening in his mouth, as he looked at the tender chapattis beginning to swell from the fresh ghee, they were bathed in.

Chapattis were the bread of India, and used to not only make sandwiches, but to scoop up the ever-sweet Basmati rice, lentils and spices that were part of their staple diet.

Right at that moment a chapatti, some fresh curried rice and spiced yogurt tea sounded like Christmas to him; and he did not celebrate Christmas. He celebrated something else.

The baker looked out his window at Gandhi and waved.

Gandhi waved back.

The baker gestured for him to come inside.

Gandhi wanted to, but he did not have the time.

He gestured to the pocket watch that hung from his neck on a golden chair. Its hands were shaped like those of a monkey. Hanuman's face was beneath the watch face numbers that denoted the hours. He was smiling.

Gandhi was not.

He was sweating.

Hard.

And not just from the weather patterns that had been afflicting Delhi and its citizens, but because he was being followed.

He did not dare divert his attention from where he was heading, and if he did so, he risked his friend's life. He was not the sort of man to willingly endanger another man's life. Not when it was his mission to safeguard them and even if it were not. He believed that all life had a purpose. So now, his mission was to fulfill that purpose. The purpose upon which he had embarked.

And at this moment, more than any other, if he were not precise, he might not endanger anyone, because he would be dead.

So, he nodded to his friend, the baker, and rushed onwards, not fast, but not slow either. His footsteps moved him closer and closer to the temple of Hanuman. He should be safe there. The priests knew him, and they also were aware of what he was running from.

They had sent him on a mission which had caused the dread souls following him to come after him in the first place.

Three shadows fell across him from the rooftop above.

He looked up.

Three smiling faces on the bodies of two men and a woman, wearing dark cloaks and turbans stared down at him. Their smiles sent shivers of horror down his spine.

They had found him!

He could go no further, or he would endanger the temple and its inhabitants. These, who had appeared, knew no mercy, and respected no religion. His only hope had been to evade them and gain the protection of his temple and be hidden well enough that they would finally give up their hunt.

He could see now that it would not have worked anyway. They were not following the laws of man. They were guided by the hand of a demon goddess, who knew neither mercy nor love.

The three above raised a knife in each of their right hands. The knives were eight inches long and serrated on one side and sharp as a razor on the other. The dread symbol of Kali shined from their knife pommels. And tattoos on their right wrist accented their devotion to the dread goddess master. A dragon's head with medusa hair and eight arms gripped their wrists and their knife pommels.

They leaped at him.

He prepared to die.

Master of the World

Later.

Harry, Conan, and Challenger sat near the windows, looking out of the massive ship's passenger compartment at the ocean below.

The waves looked like tiny stirs of water in a bathroom sink.

"Smallest wave below is topping sixty feet, and most are a hundred at this time," Jules told his friends as he entered the passenger section with a tray of hot coffee and fresh scones.

Conan and Challenger's eyes lit up. Jules had gotten the recipe from Ms. Hudson, but his special touch had made them tasty in a way she would never have thought to do.

"Cinnamon and cloves," he had explained once. "With a dash of honey."

Harry was fascinated by the power of the clouds in the sky which seemed to be paralleling their course. "How fast are we traveling, Jules?"

"Not very," Jules replied. "We have a strong head wind which is nearly a hundred miles an hour. We could rise about it, but to do so would deprive you of nature's beauty and surprises," Jules explained with his boyish smile lighting up his face. "And knowing what you gentlemen are facing..."

His face clouded a moment when his friends darted surprised looks at him. "I mean, knowing what you attempting to do, the dangers you face..."

Again, he stopped.

Conan laughed. "Jules, just give us the damned things, will you?"

Jules smiled again, the horrified look on his face vanishing, as he distributed them to his friends.

They all thanked him profusely as they grabbed their first scone to eat; mouths' watering at what they knew was coming.

Conan was about to stuff his mouth with a scone when the ship suddenly jumped upwards, causing him to stab himself in the face with the scone instead of his mouth.

Harry turned and spotted the mess on Conan's face. "Now, now, Conan scones are meant for the palette, not makeup!"

"Very funny!" Conan retorted, wiping at the sugary mess on his cheek.

Challenger chose to remain quiet. He had been quiet
for most of the trip. His left arm was still in a cast and
pained him, even though he would not admit it.

It was not healing as fast as he had hoped.

Harry had offered to use magic on the arm, but he had refused. "Too much magic, Harry. I do not want to have to rely on you every time I get a little scratch."

Harry had eyed the cast, and then shrugged. Who was he to argue with a man who was as stubborn sometimes and seemingly as dense as a rock, even if he did have one of the most brilliant minds, he had ever known besides that of Holmes?

"What is that?" Challenger asked, pointing to something odd sailing swiftly just below the surface of the storm-tossed sea.

Harry and Conan both went to the windows to look out.

Jules snorted. "Captain Nemo, more than likely. The fellow believes his vessel, the Nautilus, is swifter underwater than our Master of the World is in the air."

Then the object descended from view.

A speaker announced, "India within the hour. Be prepared for rough weather," Wells told everyone from the cockpit.

Conan looked anxious. "I thought it already was...rough?"

Jules shrugged. "Rough is a matter of timing. And right now, the timing is not so good, but do not worry, Mon Ami, our ship will manage."

Conan muttered. "Yes, but what about us?"

Jules barked with laughter and exited the passenger deck.

Conan and Challenger exchanged glances.

Harry let out a sudden gasp.

Both men turned to look at him to see what had happened.

Harry was clutching at his left hand which was on fire.

Harry screamed!

Diversion to Death

Chandni Chowk Marketplace
Temple of Kali
Old Delhi, India
Now

The structure of Delhi is unique in that it is a sprawling city, looking like most any other city, you might walk or pass through, or perhaps see pictures of in your newspaper or occasional magazine, but to live there or spend any significant amount of time in the city is another thing altogether.

It is not unusual to find temples blended into the streets of the city mostly on side streets a regular tourist might not explore for fear of being mugged by thieves or worse, have your throat slit because you were easy prey. Some of the poor were not so passive about their poverty but prayed on the weak and the trusting.

No, Delhi was not an unruly town, but it was big. One of the largest in India, except for Kolkata, which staggers the mind with its population that is so large that to walk the streets through the numerous humans there is like trying to walk through an incoming tide or breaker on the shore of the sea. There is that many people!

Carl Manchester did not worry about the size of the city. He did not give the number of poor and starving citizens a second thought at all. He was well off and he intended to be even more so by the time he returned to Europe by way of the Britains.

He smiled as he pondered his name and affluence. They were remarkable to a person listening to him. This is what he wanted. Acceptance and influence.

He had told everyone he met, after he disembarked from the large tri-balloon dirigible that had flown here from London, he had a huge sum of personal wealth in London, with which he hoped to make significant investments, here in Delhi.

It did not take long for sharks to start sniffing him out and circle him for a meal. And the biggest one of all was an Indian merchant, Kuran Seiki, a dark skinned, bellicose man who always knew where the deals were.

So, he claimed anyway.

He had a nose as large as his exaggerated view of his financial skills. Neither one of which Carl had any reason to debate at this moment as he watched with fascination a huge black fly land on Kuran's nose and begin cleaning itself there.

Kuran did not even bat an eye. He continued pointing to the alleys they passed as they walked into the marketplace and describing what they held.

The hustle and bustle of merchants, both poor and rich, was loud and clamorous for attention.

Beggars ran up to him once with hands outstretched, changing, "Baksheesh! Baksheesh!"

He had chased them off with a scattering of English pennies, which had sent them into a chaotic scramble to get as many as they can.

Kuran had grabbed his arm as he prepared to throw down some bills as well. "If you value your life, do not do this, Mister Manchester. These kinds see your miserable amount as a fortune and would slit your throat if they thought for a moment, you had more."

He hurriedly repocketed his bills without showing them.

He had not known that. He had always suspected the poverty here was tremendous. He had been here before, but he had always been with others and too preoccupied with the work he was doing to notice the extreme poverty, but momentarily, as he passed through it.

"Now," Kuran went on, pointing to a new alley. "Here, this alley leads to the temple of Vishnu."

"Vishnu?"

"The Big God, Mister Manchester. The very biggest."

Carl peered into the alley; saw a squat dirty building sandwiched between two merchant shops that looked equally as foul. But it had what looked like a golden roof.

"Evidently your god has little care for where he lives, flaunting his wealth above his home, but sharing none below." He said, after spotting several priests of the temple tossing a beggar out into the street, then cursing him and going back inside.

Kuran eyed Carl sternly. "Be careful what you say of the gods here, Mister Manchester. The people take them quite seriously."

Carl nodded but had no respect for the people's beliefs. If they wanted to believe in pagan gods, that was their loss, not his. Not that he believed anymore so in a Christian God, just that the pagan ones...such as this Vishnu...he had no respect for at all. Especially when he saw so much squalor associated with the name.

Kuran, unaware of his client's thoughts, took him a bit further and showed another alley. It was darker, longer and wound down to the marketplace situated below this part of the city. "Here is the temple of Kali."

Carl nodded again. Did not look any different than the last ten or so had, but he had to give Kuran his due. He knew his stuff, even if his nose was a bit huge and still bearing a fly at its tip.

Kuran finally noticed and swats it away.

The fly shot lazily about his head and then landed on Kuran's right ear, which was also remarkably huge. Kuran ignored it.

"And this is our destination."

Carl nodded. There was nothing to say. It looked like he had wasted his time. But looks could be deceiving. He nodded yet again. "Good."

Kuran took that as an approval of what he saw. It was not.

The Kali temple was even fouler looking than the last they had passed. It looked ready to collapse at any given moment. Several native Indians were sprawled about its entrance, sucking on Hookah pipes, their eyes shut as they contemplated whatever heaven was in their impoverished minds.

"Sad," Carl said as they passed the two men.

Kuran shrugged. "Each to his own, as you Brits say, hey, Mister Manchester?"

"Indeed."

"You asked for me to bring you to the temple of legends. That of Kali, the eight-armed goddess. This is it. I suspect it will be quite an awakening to a man of your western mind."

Carl shrugged. "I've seen a lot in my short time on this earth."

"There is always more, Mister Manchester," Kuran said as he led him forwards. "And not all of it filled with wonder and beauty."

"I've seen that part of the world too, Kuran."

Kuran stopped for a moment and gave Carl a look that caused his hair to stand up on the back of his head. "Are you so sure of that?"

Then Kuran parted a curtain of beads which ranged from the size of chickpeas to small walnuts. They were glossy and shone with all colors of the rainbow...red, orange, green, blue, mauve, and purple and so on.

The beads clinked together in a soothing sound as they entered a low lit, dank interior that seemed to stretch forever.

Carl suddenly got interested. How was this possible?"

They continued walking in silence, further and further inside, and it got darker as scones of fire lit the walkway, but barely lit the floor, which seemed to be made of tiled marble with strange designs on them that resembled creatures he'd never seen before. The light from the scone lights flickered constantly, causing shadows to dance about them as if alive.

Once, Carl had reached for the pistol he had holstered on his right hip, but Kuran had caught him before he could draw.

"Illusion. Just illusion. Light can play tricks on our minds. It has been designed here to frighten those not worthy of the mistress, Kali."

"It works," Carl replied.

And work it did. A huge shape with eight arms seemed to follow them along the walls, before they finally entered a huge chamber. He was stunned for a moment. It was the same shape he had seen following them in the corridor.

Mounted on a dais that stood almost ten feet tall was the most horrifying looking creature...female supposedly...that he had ever seen. And its skin was a deep black purple and glistening, as if it were sweating, though that was impossible. It was only stone. Wasn't it?

Carl felt the breath catch in his throat.

"Kali," Kuran said.

"She's..."

Kuran eyed Carl. "Oh, she is that and more."

Then the right arm of the statue moved, and Kali's huge eyes opened and focused on Carl.

221B Baker Street

T*hen.*

Harry sat across the table from Holmes, cradling his arms on the tabletop, while Conan sat to his right and Challenger to his left.

Holmes was examining a map quite studiously.

Watson peered at his friends from his window seat, then went back to reading the London Times morning edition.

Ms. Hudson sat next to Watson, knitting as usual, a contented look on her face.

"So, this is where you intend to start looking?" Holmes asked, stabbing a spot on the map before him.

"Exactly. Delhi."

Holmes looked up. "And you feel this is where the cult of the blood orchid sprang from."

"I do."

Holmes nodded.

Challenger leaned forward. "Jules and Wells should be arriving any minute now to fly us over the ocean to the place. They are on their way to the Americas and a slight diversion is nothing to them and their craft."

"Yes," Holmes replied with a slight smile. "That craft of theirs is unlike any other."

Conan beamed. "It has a better bathroom than that of my own house."

Watson piped in. "And kitchen."

Ms. Hudson pinched his arm. "I don't like the way you say that, John."

He smiled at her. "But not nearly as lovely as your own, of course, my dear."

"Of course," she responded. Satisfied, she returned to her knitting. A shawl for Lady Shareen, who was expected over later that evening for dinner.

Her husband, the Jungle Lord, Lord Graystone, was off into Fairie again, looking out for the dragon family he watched over there, so she had more free time to visit and was taking advantage of it.

"Sure, I can't persuade you to take me with you?" Holmes asked.

"We'd love you to," Conan spoke up.

Harry shook his head. "Not this time, Holmes. It is our investigation. If we brought you along, the Queen would think us incapable."

"I rather doubt that, Harry," Watson jumped in. "She's rather fond of you, you know."

Harry blushed.

"The same, I'd rather we performed this case ourselves," Harry insisted.

Holmes nodded and then glanced at Watson. "Well, sorry, Watson, I know how much you were looking forward to seeing the jungles there."

Watson scowled. "Yes, you and the butcher."

Harry gave Holmes a blank look.

"Watson is referring to our local butcher, who came from India's jungles."

Harry glanced over at Watson. "Not all India is jungles, Watson."

"Enough," Watson replied with a frown, indicating that as far as he was concerned this conversation was over. "If I wanted to sweat like a pig, I would have been born one. Delhi this time of year is like a baker's oven and people drop like flies from it."

Harry looked away to hide his smile. He knew the real reason Watson did not want to go was because he did not want to expose his beloved to danger. He knew Ms. Hudson well enough to know she would not let Watson go without her. She had become a regular companion to Holmes and Watson on many of their cases of late. He did not believe that would become less in the future. She was an intelligent and capable woman and not one to allow any man to hold her back from her ambitions.

A great shadow fell across the buildings outside. Watson and Ms. Hudson turned to look.

Hanging in the sky above the buildings on the opposite side of the street was a huge flying ship that resembled Captain Nemo's submarine, but without diving fins or propeller. It hovered above the building on twin beams of energy. Its massive hull was a complex weaving of gears and plates of metal.

It had both propellers, which could be collapsed for faster travel at higher speeds, and the String powered propulsor rays to power it.

"What do you call that coming from the ship's bottom, John?" Ms. Hudson asked.

"It's what powers the ship."

"Then why can we see it?"

"Because it not only powers the ship, but it propels it as well."

"What's it called?"

"Thread something or other," Watson replied with a frown. "And do not bother asking me how a thread can power a ship of that magnitude. I do not even understand how a Tesla powered car works, let alone that behemoth outside."

Ms. Hudson pressed his arm warmly and went back to her knitting. She knew he did. He was just frustrated because he was worried about the safety of his friends. This is what she loved about him the most. He was a loyal friend, and he would never endanger a friend's life unless he had to, and would never abandon them, even if it risked his own life to stay with them.

He and Sherlock were like twins in that manner. Mirrors of each other. The best and the best.

Watson watched as a hatch opened amidships as the huge vessel began to lower towards the street. It was too large to fit between the buildings, but it had an extensible ramp that could just barely reach the pavement.

Citizens on the sidewalks below all turned to look upwards as the ramp descended.

Master of the World

Later.

"For God's sake, help the man!" Challenger roared, tossing a tumbler of water on Harry's hand.

Conan was about to do the same, but Harry warded him off with a gesture of his free hand, shut his eyes and then said. "Finis!"

The red fire surrounding his right hand vanished.

Harry collapsed to the floor.

Gandhi

Chandni Chowk Marketplace
Old Delhi, India

Now

Gandhi, without even giving it a second thought or even a first, flipped his pocket watch open with his thumb and thrust it at the descending Kali followers.

"Hanuman!" He cried out. "Help me!"

A brilliant flash of light burst in the air nearby, flooding the three falling thugs with a brilliant, but golden flare of light.

When his eyes lost the glare from them, he found himself alone.

He turned about to see what had caused the flash, expecting to see Hanuman with his rod of justice ready to dispense punishment.

It was not. He sighed with relief. He was not so sure if he was ready to meet Hanuman after all.

The Master of the World had just started descending and its golden hull had caught the light of the sun and reflected it brilliantly across the city. He leaned back to see it more clearly.

It was so massive that it filled the sky.

Indians about him were all shouting and gesturing at the strange vessel as it lowered towards the ground. Bursts of blue light came from the bottom of the ship and its rear. It began to slow and then dropped to a hover over Delhi Square, which was part of Chandni Chowk Marketplace, a huge marketplace where merchants gathered to sell everything from highly polished semi-precious stones on necklaces and bracelets to the more sophisticated and graceful, but extremely colorful saris that women wore.

He ran towards the marketplace.

Not because the ship was landing there and he was curious, but because it was the meeting place. The exact place he had been fleeing towards.

It was landing right where he was supposed to meet a man. A man of great power. One who could help him and his people free themselves of the evil Cult of the Blood Orchid, the followers of Kali the eight-armed goddess.

He should have been paying better attention to what was going on around him.

He got to within ten yards of the craft and it was lowering a ramp.

Three men stepped into the hatch where the ramp was descending from.

Then something struck him from behind.

Darkness consumed him!

The Hands of Kali

*Chandni Chowk Marketplace
Old Delhi, India
Temple of Kali
Now*

Carl felt something odd, not from just the statue, although that had his hair standing up on end, it was much closer. More imminent.

He would never be able to explain why later, but he suddenly dropped to the floor, his intuition screaming at him to do so. So, he had.

That was when he felt a man stumble over him, then scream as he struck the floor.

Carl turned over and saw Kuran laying there. He was struggling to get up but could not. He watched the man die before his eyes, knowing he was helpless to save him.

Carl saw the jagged knife blade sticking from Kuran's back. But the knife was coming from the other side out his back. He had been trying to stab Carl and had fallen on his own deadly blade.

A pool of blood began to course from beneath Kuran's body and as it did so, it did not just pool there and stop. It kept on flowing like something alive. Towards the statue of Kali.

Carl knew Kuran was dead that moment, but he did not know what was going to happen next and he had no intentions of finding out either when he heard others moving into the room. Between the blood that had a life of its own, the bestial Kali statue that had a life of its own and his near death, he had had enough of this place.

He managed to leap to his feet. He then sprinted not away from Kali as a wise man normally might have, but towards it. Her eyes widened and her mouth opened eagerly to consume him, revealing sharp, and dagger like teeth.

He heard the men rushing into the room, spotting Kuran on the floor. They did not sound an alarm, yell, scream or draw attention to themselves. They just kept moving. Towards Carl.

The hand of Kali was descending towards him. Her lower right hand. It was so close he could feel the air flow from it smashing towards his skull. But instead of being flattened by the living statue, he used the acrobatic skills he had learned as a kid over ten years ago and leaped upwards, swinging over the hand, onto the arm, and then springing to the next arm and then the next.

As he made the incredibly strange, bizarre series of leaps, knives flew, just missing him. Only his constant movement kept him safe. He did not think, he just acted.

He reached the top arm, ran up to her shoulder. Her head turned to look at him. She smiled, revealing just how long and deadly her dagger teeth were. They were gruesome dagger length teeth that were aged with mold and rot.

"Sorry, Miss, but I've got a date with someone with better hygiene," he told Kali, then used her nose to throw himself onto her head and then from there he leaped onto the overhead cross beam that arched upwards towards a crystal dome high overhead.

As he ran more knives flew at him, leaving a trail of quivering blades where he had stepped last.

Finally, he made one mighty leap, smashing upwards towards the glass dome, praying it was not as solid as it looked.

Master of the World

B*efore*
"Harry, for God's sake, man wake up!"

"Conan, fetch some more water," Challenger ordered.

"On it," Conan replied.

"Stop!"

Conan and Challenger both looked at Harry, who was sitting up by himself, staring at his burnt right hand. He pressed his left hand over it, shut his eyes and then his head seemed to glow a soft green a moment.

A flood of soothing, green energies flowed from his forehead down his arm and onto his hand and over both. He held the pose, allowing the flood to continue for several long minutes, then he opened his eyes again and the light vanished.

He held his hand up.

It was perfectly healed.

Harry reached up and Challenger gave him a hand.

"You really had us worried, Harry."

"Me too," Harry said with a grin. "I wasn't expecting it this time either."

"What's it means?"

The Master of the World violently jolted a moment.

Jules grinned at his friends. "What it means is that we are landing."

The three men followed Jules to the hatch.

Wells met them there.

"Who's flying the ship?" Conan asked fearfully.

"It's on automatic."

"Automatic?" Conan blurted out in horror. "You mean no one is piloting us?"

"No one alive, Conan," Wells said with a grin. He slapped Conan on his shoulder. "Do not worry, old man, we are well cared for. Even if they are...uh...shall we say...somewhat mechanical."

The ship settled and seemed to bobble a moment, then Wells, and Jules unlatched the hatch and threw it open.

The ramp automatically began dropping towards the marketplace below.

And that is when they saw Gandhi looking up at them and the man rushing him from behind.

Challenger was fast on the draw, but not fast enough. He fired twice. The man with the knife struck Gandhi on the head with his knife as he fell, instead of stabbing him in the back as intended.

The other two fled to the left and right of Gandhi, but instead of attacking as they had planned, they fled into the alley on the right, even as a crowd of Indians roared with anger and began throwing things at the remaining two.

"Seems we have done a bit of good already, my good man," Wells said to Jules.

"Mon Ami, we are always doing more than a bit of good everywhere we go," Jules added.

They laughed, and then began walking the ramp downwards, followed by the others.

A Smashing Presentation

Chandni Chowk Marketplace
Temple of Kali
Old Delhi, India
Now

SMASH!

CRACKLE!

No.

It was not as thick as he feared. He did not plunge back into the Kali temple to his death. But the glass cut in dozens of places as he broke through it, struck the rim of the vast glass overhang, and rolled safely onto the hard baked roof.

He lay there a moment, too stunned to even take a breath. He really needed to stop getting out like this. Finally, with a great will of effort, he rolled onto his side, t hen his back. He looked up and saw the huge Master of the World floating there.

Interesting!

Then he felt, and then heard grapple hooks catching the rim of the broken window metal frame and the sound of men and women screaming angrily as they poured up the ropes they had flung to capture and kill him.

He groaned.

"No rest for the wicked," he sighed.

He jumped to his feet, staggered a moment, caught a glimpse of the tears all over his pants, shirt, hands and probably his neck and scalp as well, because he felt a slow ooze dribble down the back of his neck and onto his forehead.

He swiped at his forehead.

Blood!

He needed to see a doctor soon.

This was not exactly the cleanest of places he had been to lately.

Then the sound of screams, even louder than before, and the first hands reaching the edge of the broken glass came into view.

He stepped on a few fingers and listened to the pleasurable sound of screams as the wounded fell.

He took no pride in doing so, but he also was not a fool. These were out to murder him. No questions asked.

He had been a fool to trust Kuran. The man had seemed just a bit too knowledgeable from the start. He sighed again unhappily, tucked his shirt back in, rushed to the edge of the roof and gauged the distance to the ground.

Too far.

He would probably break his legs, or at the least his ankles if he jumped.

Then he heard bodies rolling onto the roof behind him.

Drats!

He jumped.

Gandhi

C*handni Chowk Marketplace*
Old Delhi, India

Now

Gandhi rushed to Challenger and began shaking his hand vigorously. "Thank you! Thank you! Thank you!"

Conan grinned.

Harry smiled.

Jules and Wells remained on the lip of the ramp, watching patiently, but with a hint of something distant in them, as if they were watching a movie that they had already seen.

Harry turned to them. For a moment he paused upon the look he saw on their faces, and then he shrugged it off as to fatigue, "I think we can handle it from here. I'll give you a hand," he said waving his right hand comically, "...when we need you again."

Jules grinned. "It's always fun seeing your magic working, Harry."

Harry looked at his right hand. "And a big thank you God that it still is, the way that fire caught me off guard yet again!"

Jules shrugged. "The future is not ours to see, Mon Ami."

He gave Wells a quick mysterious glance, and then turned a smile on Harry again.

Wells shook Harry's hand. "We will stay close. Got a few things to do ourselves while we are here."

Jules and Wells exchanged mysterious looks again, and then climbed the ramp back into the Master of the World.

Before Wells shut the hatch, he gave Harry a short wave, but somehow Harry felt as if the wave meant much, much more than just a simple goodbye until we see each other again.

Wells look was lost as the ramp withdrew back into the ship, the hatch shut and the Master of the World about ten seconds later began to rise, like a giant behemoth of the sea, but in the sky.

The Indians gathered about the men all gasped in awe, shouted, and pointed, excited about the magnificent craft.

Challenger brought Gandhi forward. "Gentlemen, I'd like you to meet the friend we came for."

Gandhi put his hands together and said, "Namaste!"

Then the crowds about Challenger and his friends all let out shouts of fear and scrambled for safety, leaving a circle of Kali thugs surrounding them, knives raised.

Sharp, serrated knives.

Harry smiled. "I guess we've found the source of the Blood Orchid Cult."

Challenger shook his head. "Look closer."

Harry did, as did Conan. The wrists of the men and women surrounding them did not have the deadly tattoo on them.

Harry looked at Challenger. "Then why are they threatening us?"

Gandhi looked at his feet nervously.

"Gandhi!" Challenger roared.

Gandhi gave the men an apologetic look, and then pulled out a huge jewel with the figure of Kali in the center of it.

"Oh, give me a break," Challenger roared.

The Kali thugs saw the jewel and let out a cry of anger and hatred.

"Sorry," Gandhi whispered.

"If we live long enough to accept it, maybe I'll consider it," Challenger growled, then readied his weapon.

The Kali thugs charged them, bloodlust, and anger in their eyes and on their faces!

Wagon of Good Luck

Chandni Chowk Marketplace
Old Delhi, India
Now

Carl cartwheeled as he fell, trying to aim himself at the canvas heaped below in a large cart that was slowly moving away from the building. The cart loomed closer and closer.

He was not going to make it.

Then someone darted in front of the cart, holding a huge knife in their hands.

The elephant drawing the cart trumpeted in alarm and hurriedly backed up, rising on its rear feet.

Carl landed on his back on the canvas with a loud smack.

The elephant dropped to its front feet, startled by the sound, and smashed into the Kali thug who had been rushing to finish off Carl if he survived the jump.

Carl did.

The Kali thug did not.

The elephant backed up from the broken body beneath its right foot and let out another loud trumpeting sound.

Carl slid off the cart, gave the driver a salute of thanks, then ran towards the marketplace.

The Master of the World began to rise.

He did not' stop.

Behind him the sound of the Kali cult grew, and he glanced over his shoulder. They were pouring from the front entrance of the temple like a swarm of angry bees from a disturbed nest.

And every one of them had a knife.

Long and serrated.

"Oh crap!" He cursed and then put on more speed.

Marketplace

*Chandni Chowk Marketplace
      Old Delhi, India*

Now

"TAKE IT!" Challenger roared and hurled the precious Kali jewel into the air.

Every single one of the charging Kali thugs stopped to watch the jewel as it turned end over end in the air.

Challenger rushed the nearest, followed by the others, shouldered them aside and kept running.

Entrance to the Marketplace

Chandni Chowk Marketplace
Old Delhi, India

Now

Carl did not slow down, even though his chest was burning from the intensity of his run and lack of air to replenish what he was breathing out. His legs and arms hurt. His entire body was a temple of aches and pains.

He dodged first about a huge caravan of camels that was lugging huge clay jars, undoubtedly filled with dates and oils. Then he ducked under another elephant that was in his path, racing beneath its harness, the elephant ignorant of his passing.

He swerved hard left to get behind a series of stalls where various dyed clothes were hung up to reveal their achingly beautiful colors of the rainbow. He heard a scream.

He looked back.

Two of the Kali thugs had tried to replicate his dash and were stepped on by the elephant.

But the others kept on running, dodging around the huge beast and the burden it carried.

He was not losing them at all.

Then he got an idea.

The heavily gated entrance to the marketplace was close. It had a double set of large iron and wood structures to shut off the area. It was a left over from an earlier period in India when it was divided and at war.

If he could make it to them in time, he could manually shut them, God willing they were not rusted open on their hinges and then make it deeper into Delhi and lose the bastards chasing him.

He reached the gates and eyed the massive doors.

How was he going to do this?

Then he heard a shout of triumph behind him. He had been spotted.

He turned about to face the dozens of Kali thugs chasing towards him.

Then he heard another thunderous rising of cries. He turned about to find Challenger, Harry, Conan, and Gandhi racing towards him from the other direction.

But not to help him, to save their own butts!

They were being chased by a horde of angry Kali thugs with even bigger knives than the ones chasing him.

Drat!

Sanity during Insanity

Chandni Chowk Marketplace
Old Delhi, India

Now

"Who are you?" Harry demanded of Carl as he reached him.

"I could ask the same, but being as we are both about to die, I'll save it for later." Carl replied with a grin.

He turned about to face the horde rushing from his direction.

"Agreed," Harry said and turned with his friends to face the horde of Kali thugs coming from their direction.

Harry eyed the huge doors.

"Two choices."

"Both bad," Challenger replied, getting the drift of what Harry was thinking.

"For God's sake, Harry, just do it!" Conan hollered.

Harry raised his right hand.

Both the Kali thug groups saw the raised hand.

"Whoops!" Gandhi said. "That is a grave insult to the Kali worshippers.

"What does it mean?" Conan asked innocently.

"That they won't stop now until they've sliced every inch of our skin off our backs and torn our organs out to feed to the ants."

The Kali Thugs rushed even faster!

"I wondered why they seemed so suddenly more aggressive," Conan groaned.

Challenger grinned. "You've already died once; how lucky do you want to be anyway?"

Conan sighed, and then raised his weapon to face the rushing horde. He could see into their eyes now. He saw no pity or remorse for what they were planning...their death!

He only saw visions of himself torn apart and littering the filthy streets of the marketplace.

"Damn!" He and Carl cursed at the same time.

221B Baker Street

Holmes thumbed through the pages of the London Times, his eyes scanning for details.

Watson was doing the same with the Morning Herald.

Ms. Hudson came into the room with a fresh pot of coffee and steaming scones.

"Snack anyone?"

Watson threw down his paper in disgust. "Nothing. Dratted nothing!"

He glanced over at Ms. Hudson, who was startled by his outburst. "Not you, my dear, this blasted paper. Nothing in it of import."

He rose to help her set the table for the three of them, while Holmes continued his scanning, finishing a page, flipping it over, then ripping it out of the bundle and tossing it to the floor.

Ms. Hudson spotted a huge pile of newspaper litter beside Holmes's chair, standing about three feet tall. "Let me guess, every paper in town, plus the ones from everywhere else as well?"

Watson nodded. "And nothing. Not one blasted word about the blaggarts behind all the murders."

Holmes finished his last page, but instead of tossing it, folded it into a neat box shape, then folded it over again and tucked it into his shirt pocket. He rose.

"Come, Watson, we have a lead."

Watson grabbed several scones and folded them into a napkin, went to the coat rack and stuffed them into his coat pocket as he slipped his coat on.

"What kind? And where?"

"The Morgue."

Watson gave Ms. Hudson a roll of his eyes. "Of course. Where else!"

Ms. Hudson came over and gave Watson a quick hug. "Go get them, grumbly bear!"

He started to protest, then leaned forward and gave her a sweet peck on the cheek.

He turned to speak to Holmes, but the man was already scurrying down the stairs.

Watson sighed. It was Midnight already. Another night without a proper sleep.

Then he smiled and thought to himself *"I'll bet Harry and the others are having themselves a grand old time in India."*

Marketplace Entrance

Chandni Chowk Marketplace
Old Delhi, India

Now

An explosion of blue fire lit up Harry's right hand and his entire body, so that he looked like a mythical striding the Earth to wreak vengeance and havoc.

The Kali thugs stopped charging on both sides.

Harry gave them a theatrical grin he had learned from William Shakespeare that he would use just before he was about to do a deadly trick. "I am death; I am come for you!" He shouted at them.

The Kali thugs on both sides flung themselves about and ran as fast as their feet could carry them. Some fell and were trampled on. They got back up and stumbled after the others, until not a one was left.

The King Andrews Hotel

"**I** never thought I'd be happy to hear that name again," Challenger remarked as he looked up at the name of the hotel they were checking into: The King Andrews Hotel.

Conan chuckled. "Fate has a way of reminding us of many things, Challenger, both good...and bad."

Harry took a deep breath and glanced at Gandhi and Carl, who were chatting near the entrance to the hotel, glancing their way as they spoke.

"And if you're lucky enough to have weathered all of them, you're the wiser for it."

"Or dead," Challenger added.

"Or dead," Harry laughed. "And thank God that miserable tyrant is dead, for our country has enough on its plate without adding a dark and evil King to it."

The hotel clerk handed Harry the key to their room. He clapped his hands twice and two bell hops came running up.

Harry smiled. "Sorry, old chap, but we haven't any luggage."

The hotel clerk was about to send off the two bell hops, who looked upset that they would not be getting a tip after all, when Conan pulled out a pound note and flattened it on the desk. "Split it between the two of them, will you, sir?"

The hotel clerk smiled and nodded.

Harry headed for the stairs.

"Well played, Conan."

The two bell hops and the hotel clerk were fighting over the tip, over which would get more or what amount then.

"My wager is on the hotel clerk getting half of it," Challenger said with a grin.

"Won't take you up on that one, Challenger," Conan replied. "I've been to India before."

Harry laughed. "It's not so different from London."

"Actually..." Challenger added, "...It is. In London they serve tea and cakes as they argue."

The three men burst into laughter and went ahead up the stairs.

Carl and Gandhi followed several moments later.

But unknown to any of them, one of the Indian porters who stood silently at the door turned to watch them vanish up the stairs.

On his right wrist was the symbol of Kali.

Room 221B

"Simply remarkable," Harry commented as he sat down on a plush chair at a small mahogany table that was set already with a bright, white cover with tiny mandalas woven in an assortment of colors on its edges.

Several plates of food sat in its center. The middle one had fresh pears and dates. The other was covered.

Challenger uncovered it and revealed a huge mound of Basmati rice with saffron liberally sprinkled over it, and a stack of chapattis, steaming from fresh, hot ghee that had been buttered lavishly upon them.

"Dinner is served, gentlemen," Conan announced.

Carl and Gandhi pulled up chairs, as did Conan and Challenger.

They ate quietly for a time, all famished from the brief fighting and fleeing they had been forced to do, as well as by the tumultuous turns of danger and possible loss of life they had been facing since they entered India.

They were brave men; but even brave men get upset stomachs when facing or in the middle of battle. No one really likes the idea of dying.

Some brag they are fearless but beg for another minute when their time comes.

Finally, finished, they began yawning.

Harry turned about, surveying the rest of the room.

"Carl, you and Gandhi can have the adjoining room, Conan and Challenger you can have the large bed and I'll sleep on the couch."

"This is going to be a long night," Challenger said pointedly, eyeing the distinctively rough looking wooden sofa with a spread of cotton blankets covering it in a colorful panoply of mandala patterns.

"I'm used to it," Harry replied. "At least I won't have to listen to the avalanche of snores that Conan does when he sleeps."

"Hey, that's not very gentlemanly of you," Conan shot at him.

"Please forgive me, Conan. The gentle avalanche of snores," Harry amended.

Conan snorted but said nothing further.

Nor did anyone else. They were all too tired to argue further or fight about who should be the bigger gentleman.

Carl and Gandhi went into their room to settle down for the night.

Challenger and Conan lie on the larger bed and shut their eyes. Both men fell asleep almost at once.

Harry, however, was not.

He got up from the sofa, went to the adjoining room's door, and opened it.

Carl sat up from the bed he and Gandhi were sharing and nodded.

Rooftop Menace

"And that's how I ended up in that hellish situation," Carl explained, sighing with relief to finally get his explanation out and over with. He could tell it was bothering Harry and wanted to tell him sooner, but Harry kept giving obvious signals to wait.

Harry, hands clasped behind his back in thought, sat on the edge of the rooftop, which was built up about three feet from the heavily graveled rooftop of hand laden bricks and looked out over Old Delhi.

In the distance he could see the Ganges, its waters reflecting the bright moon that hung overhead like a huge white pearl. Even at this distance he could hear the thunder of its waters as it rushed along its riverbanks.

In many ways it felt comfortable to him; it reminded him of the Thames.

"So," he finally managed, turning to look at Carl, who stood next to him, his face pensive, lips tightly locked together.

"The Secret Service?"

"Yes," Carl agreed. "Officially, we don't exist and if I didn't already know you and your friends didn't have the highest of security clearances from our Good Queen Mary of Scots, I'd have to kill you."

Harry grinned. "Or try."

Carl grinned back. "Or try."

"But I've never failed," Carl added.

Harry smiled gently, but sternly. "Always the first time, old chap."

Carl let out a deep sigh. "How have we ended up with this? I just wanted to get everything straight with you, not make this a battle of wills!"

Harry nodded. "Gentleman's agreement then?"

"Agreed. Just business at hand."

Harry looked back over the city again. "What don't I understand is why the Queen didn't inform us of your activities here?"

"You know her as well as I do, Harry."

He gave Harry a wink. "And some say, better."

Harry blushed but did not deny it.

Carl's eyes widened. "Well then..."

"Please, don't let my relationships stop you from enlightening me, Inspector."

Carl gave him a surprised look. Harry pointed to the badge just inside Carl's coat that had slipped into view.

"Oh, well then, I suppose you should also know that my name is not Carl, but Inspector Wilde, Angus Wilde. I work for the top echelon of our country, or to put it bluntly..."

"For the Queen," Harry finished for him.

"Exactly."

"So, what is it she expects from you, but not from me?"

"Whether we are to invade India or not."

Harry was startled by this information. He almost lost his balance.

Inspector Wilde smiled. "Easy now, Harry. The Queen would never forgive me if my bluntness caused your untimely demise."

Harry dropped from the ledge to stand instead. This day had been trying, but the added information he was receiving was testing him greatly.

"Very well, the whole truth is out then."

"Not quite, Harry," Inspector Wilde explained.

"The whole truth is..."

Before he could say both men were alarmed by the shape of huge shadows falling across t hem from the bright moonlight.

They turned to look as ten men and women with blood red eyes charged them, their hands clutching blood red knives that glowed with fire.

Room 221B

Challenger rubbed at his left ear. Conan's head moved slightly and then his hair brushed Challenger's ear again.

Finally, Challenger groaned and got off the bed.

Conan did not even notice. He just kept snoring.

Challenger sighed, slipped into his shoes again, then his jacket and headed for the door.

He clutched the handle and opened it.

"Hello!" He said, startled.

A huge Kali thug and five smaller ones stood there with knives, blood red knives, grinning at him.

Rooftop Menace

"Jump!" Harry commanded, leaping onto the rooftop ledge. "I'll catch you."

"Are you crazy?" Inspector Wilde shouted at him. "We are ten stories high! Who will catch you?

"Suit yourself then, Inspector." Harry dove from the edge and vanished from view.

Inspector Wilde reached into his jacket for his weapon and then realized he had not worn it to the rooftop.

"Bollix!" He cursed.

He spun about, the lead Kali thug closing on him. He kicked the man in his privates. The man tumbled back, grabbing at his crotch, but the ones behind him, spilled to the left and right and charged forward, ignoring the pain of their comrade. They were followed by two more.

"Oh, drat it all anyhow!" Inspector Wilde cursed, and then he leaped onto the ledge and jumped off.

Room 221 B

Challenger slammed the door shut in the faces of the attackers, latched it, and then screamed. "Everyone out the window! Now!"

Conan coughed awake and gazed about him, stunned by the sudden interruption of his sleep.

"Where's Harry?"

"No time!" Challenger roared, flinging open the only window in the room. "Hurry or die!"

The door was struck hard from the other side and its top hinge loosened so that it hung ajar.

"Oh God!" Conan cried out.

Challenger struck the screen from the open window and then pulled himself through it. He spied a ledge below that was just wide enough. He stepped onto it, then reached a hand back inside.

"Conan, hurry!"

"I'm afraid of heights!"

"Not a good time to be afraid," Challenger roared back.

"Any time's a good time," Conan countered, but stepped out.

He made the mistake of looking down.

He began to fall.

Free Fall

Inspector Wilde plunged like a falling rock. The pavement below, still filled with hundreds of citizens awake and going about their nocturnal tasks, were not even aware he was about to fall into them.

Then something caught him by the waist, and he slowed.

"You're heavier than you look, Inspector," Harry joked.

Inspector Wilde managed to turn slightly and saw Harry holding him by his waist. "But who's holding you up?"

Harry grinned. "No one."

The Inspector screamed like a mad man as he and Harry suddenly began falling towards the pavement below.

The Ledge of Doom

Conan gasped for breath, his heart thundering in his chest. Challenger had him clasped hard against the hotel wall and had kept his feet from falling free by the force of his pressure.

"Thanks!"

"Thank me properly when we get off this blinking death walk!" Challenger roared.

He let go of Conan, and gently urged him to walk forward. Conan did so, but this time did not look down. Instead, he felt ahead of him with his feet before he put one down.

"Turn coming, Conan," Challenger warned.

Conan nodded and then felt for the turn with his right hand. He felt the edge of the corner of the building and began edging about it. He reached it and peered about it before going further.

He froze.

"Why in the blooming hell are you stopping?" Challenger demanded, almost losing his balance from Conan's abrupt stop.

Conan eyed the upheld blood red knives that were marching in the hands of the Kali thugs edging along the ledge towards him.

"Let's just say that we have a wee bit of company, and let it go at that."

Then Challenger heard commotion behind him. He turned slightly and saw a motion of up flung blood red knives coming towards him in the hands of more Kali thugs.

"Blast it all, Conan, if we didn't have bad luck, we'd have none at all about now."

"I heartily agree, Challenger."

Conan reached into his jacket and pulled out his weapon. He grimaced at the wild-eyed man leading the pack at him. "Unless you'd like to die first, I'd suggest an alternative route."

The Kali thug stopped suddenly at the sight of the gun.

His abrupt stop caused the man before him to lose his balance. He fell sideways, clutched at the man who had just stopped and took him over the side as well.

Their screams broke the silence of the night.

The other Kali thugs ignored their deaths and rushed forward.

Never So Sweet

Inspector Wilde stopped screaming when his feet touched the ground as lightly as a feather. He gave Harry an astounded look. "You really do, do magic."

Harry did not reply. His eyes were on the top floor where Challenger and Conan were on the ledge.

Blood Orchid Thugs

Challenger and Doyle put their backs to each other and began firing their weapons.

One Kali thug after another tumbled from the ledge to their deaths, but more kept taking their places.

"I'm down to my last two bullets, Challenger."

"So am I."

They eyed the remaining Kali thugs, which seemed as many as before.

"Do you believe in miracles, Conan?"

"Not really."

"Ever been tortured to death?"

"Not lately."

Conan reached a hand out. "I just want you to know that is it been a pleasure knowing you. Maybe in our next life things will be different."

"I do not believe in next lives. I like this one too much," Challenger said with a grin.

"Thank you," Conan said, his eyes watering with pride in the man standing next to him.

"And you, my dear, dear friend," Challenger said, his own eyes watering.

Then both men spun about to fire their last two bullets.

When the last was fired, they hurled their weapons into the face of the next attacker.

"Now, Conan?"

"What better time, Challenger?"

He and Challenger charged the Kali thugs.

Conan knocked the first one off the ledge, but the next one struck his right arm with his blade and the second struck him on his left shoulder.

Conan staggered back from the pain, but slugged the first one and he fell off, but the second one grinned and grabbed Conan, then tossed them both off the ledge.

Challenger heard Conan's scream and turned to try and stop him from falling. He rushed to catch him and barely did, but the weight was too much, and they both tumbled towards certain death below.

In the near distance a Christian church's bell began to ring MidBells.

The Master of the World

"Now!" Wells cried out as he watched the secondhand strike twelve on his control dashboard chronometer.

Jules lit up the String Engines of the Master of the World and if anyone had been below them at the time they flew over the ocean, they would have seen the massive ship become wrapped into colliding bolts of lightning in dazzling rainbows of colorful lights, then vanish.

Miracle

Challenger and Conan fell hard, faster, and faster, but neither screamed.

Then everything went black for a moment, and they found themselves lying on the deck of the passenger compartment of the Master of the World.

Wells stood there with his arms crossed.

"If you only knew how many laws of physics, we broke to save your miserable lives," Wells said.

Food for Thought

"And yet again, you cheated death, Conan," Challenger told his friend at the dining table inside the massive Master of the World.

Conan nodded. Gandhi had not made it. They had thought him safe in his room away from them; he had not been. When they had gone back later to see to him, they found blood stains on the bed. And much blood on the floor.

The bastards must have sliced him to pieces like they always did their victims, and then dragged his body away for whatever evil purpose they had in mind.

So even though the men were all in seeming good spirits, underlying that tone of comradery was the knowledge that they had failed a fellow comrade. Even though they had not known him long, or even much about him, they were the kind of men who saw loss of life as personal, not something to be dismissed because it happened all the time.

They were in the business of saving lives; and when they failed, it grieved them deeply. But it is to their good credit, that despite this sense of loss they did not want to weigh each other's hearts down more than they already were by dwelling on what they could not undo.

Jules spooned out huge gobbets of fresh chicken stew into the bowls of all the men at the table, and then went back to the gallery to grab the biscuits and scones he had made for dinner.

Inspector Wilde, still in shock from all the wonders he had experienced in the last twenty-four hours, and the thrashing he had taken from his plunge to certain doom, eyed Harry.

"Is it always this edge of the seat, pants on fire kind of thing for you fellows?"

Harry smiled.

Challenger roared with laughter.

Conan sipped at his stew, and then ate a chunk of chicken. He dabbed at his mustache to get the wet stew from it, and then eyed the Inspector. "What do you think?"

"I think the lot of you blaggarts are blinking out of your minds, is what I think!" He exclaimed, but with a smile on his lips.

Jules returned with the biscuits. And scones. He set them down, and then sat next to Wells, who shoved a plate over for him to eat from as well as a freshly filled bowl of stew.

Jules slid the bowl that had been before him in front of an empty chair.

"Believe me, Inspector..."

"Wilde...Angus Wilde," the Inspector told him.

"Inspector Wilde," Jules went on. "These men have faced more danger than any man in this world I know..."

"Except us of course," Wells said with a grin.

"Wells!" Jules scolded him.

Wells shrugged.

"The short of it is, that they are brave and deserve to be acknowledged by the Queen for their service," Jules finished.

"And they have been and will be again once we return to London and I can catch her ear again."

"Oh, that shan't be a problem at all, Inspector," Queen Mary's voice spoke from the door to the dining room.

Everyone turned to look in surprise.

She was dressed in rugged clothing with a pith helmet on her head, a pistol on her right hip, a huge knife on her left thigh, boots on her feet and white fatigues and shirt.

The men all at once rose, and half bowed.

She giggled. "Oh, please now. Really? Here?"

The men blushed and sat back down. She sat next to Harry and patted his right hand affectionately. "How are you, Harry?"

"Safe. For now," he told her with a smile.

She nodded and turned to survey the faces of the other men, who were not eating now. "I can only assume that since you are all here with my good friends, Jules and Wells, we have much more on our plate than any of us expected."

"Oh, so much more," Inspector Wilde agreed.

"At first I thought this would be a simple reconnoiter mission for the lot of you," she said with a smile on her lips, "But once Wells and Jules took me on a tiny jaunt into the future..."

Challenger's eyes widened. "That's how you knew!" He accused Wells and Jules, who both grinned and then gave half bows to him.

Queen Mary giggled again. "Just like old times, hey boys?"

Before they could answer, she turned to Conan. "Oh, and your wife sends her love, Conan."

He blushed.

She turned to Harry. "And Holmes has a message for you. I suspect you will find it most interesting."

"What's it about?" Conan asked.

She smiled at him and then rose, unfolded a piece of paper she had tucked into the upper right pocket of her fatigue shirt. She then read them Sherlock Holmes message.

221B Baker Street

B*efore.*
"And so, in conclusion, I feel that our only course of action has now been clearly defined for us. I trust that once you have heard my message that you will all feel equally as I about the uttermost importance of it."

Holmes stopped, bit his lower lip a moment, and then completed his message.

"Most sincerely, Sherlock Holmes!"

He folded the paper and placed it into an envelope and then set it in the center of the table.

Ms. Hudson and Watson had been quiet as he composed the letter.

Ms. Hudson finally spoke up. "Oh dear, all this drama and trauma is making me hungry."

Watson smiled. "And I."

He rose, offered his arm and she took it. Watson smiled at Holmes. "Well, since hell awaits us on the morrow, shall we at least dine on quality food this night? I know a lovely little diner that stays open after MidBells..." He said as he and Ms. Hudson went to the coat rack.

Watson put on his coat and hat and helped Ms. Hudson into hers that she had placed there earlier in the day after she had returned from shopping with a message from the Queen, which Holmes had just replied to.

She nodded to Watson, and they turned to Holmes, who remained seated.

"Sherlock!" She called to him.

Holmes looked up, his face creased with lines of worry a moment, and then he nodded, gave a warm smile, and rose to join them.

After putting on his cap and coat, he followed them downstairs to the front door.

Watson opened it and the men waited for Ms. Hudson to exit first, then followed.

On the street they turned to the left.

"It's a bit far though," Watson said, as if continuing his prior conversation.

Holmes took in a deep breath of fresh air. "Oh, I think a lovely stroll is well in order to go along with a warm meal, Watson."

Watson smiled and the three of them headed for the diner, chatting softly and often as they shared their thoughts, hopes and dreams.

Three friends on a mission of comfort before the storm of war befell upon them.

The shadow of death and destruction might be looming, but for this night, it was stricken from their thoughts as they went ahead to a well-earned meal and some well spent time together.

RADIANCE

Incident: The Impossible World

Overhead the double moons turned slowly about one another as they orbited the planet. Stars poked holes in the sky with blazing points of light. Clouds, heavy with moisture, drooped tired and weary over the ancient city of London.

A once proud city, it no longer was. It was dilapidated and beaten down.

Torn by the forces of the Goddess this world has seen better times, better ages.

Now it was a vortex of crime, monsters of the dark and men and women with evil motives.

No longer the proud London that she knew as a child. In less than twenty years it had collapsed into the ruined city it had become, with enforcers like her being trained from early childhood to help fight and resist the ever-expanding web of evil that existed these days.

And they were losing the battle.

She had seen friend after friend pass into history, their names never to be spoken on a tongue again, because even that had denied them.

Enforcers were heroes to be sure. But their names were kept private to protect their loved ones. Loved ones who would one day wake up to find the secret Enforcer gone from their world forever. Lost in the mists of time and death.

Those dark thoughts shot through her mind as she plunged headlong the length of the abandoned boardwalk. While tourists still came, they were usually heavily guarded, and once the guards were gone, so were the shop keepers and the populace.

Only the lowest of lives existed along the boardwalk at night and...her. Trying to put to right what was wrong.

But evidently failing as she gasped for air. She was closely followed by two Friskmen. Giant men who looked like a cross between catfish and humans.

They were indeed from the sea itself and had invaded her land, not overtly at first, but covertly. They were shape shifters. Something that she and her friends had not foreseen, nor expected on any level whatsoever.

And they were the reason London had fallen. Not all at once, but little by little as the monsters infiltrated London society and slowly dissected it from the inside out.

It was funny to her as her dazed mind ran through the scenarios that had led to this point in time and her life. Funny, that so many supernatural events existed from before time, but no one had known about the Friskmen.

Yes, everyone knew about vampires. She smiled. She did any way.

And there were werewolves and shape shifters of all sorts.

But shape shifting fish? Impossible, but there it was. An alien being of human intelligence but not shifting from human to a fish shape, but from fish to man.

Were they native to this world?

She did not know.

No one did.

Anyone who had gotten close to them had died. Even as she might if she could not escape them now.

Their first public appearance had been in Parliament, when the King was preparing to declare peace with France. A country Britain had been at war with for centuries.

A war that had kept both countries in an almost barbaric state. Yes, they had still made scientific progress, but crude machines that ran on physical power were hardly the kind of advancement that their citizens expected. Nor reached for.

Both nations had pretty much bombed each other's resources into nothing.

It was only when the King of England had fallen in love with the Queen of France that everything began to change.

At once, they ceased hostilities between their nations. Both had looked to cool down hot heads. And to some degree it had worked.

Until the two royals discovered that another hand was in the game besides their own. One that manipulated the populace and the government.

The Friskmen.

Even as the two nations united in the love of the King and Queen, they were carefully being dismantled by a series of sabotages that turned brother against brother, husband against wife.

The Friskmen.

That had pushed the newly united royal couple to form a secret society of warriors. Enforcers. Those people would find and discover the shape shifted humans who were Friskmen and destroy them.

She spotted her destination, and her thoughts at once ran to what to do next.

She looked over her shoulder and her pursuers were still in sight.

She only had a matter of a few seconds to get inside the nearing power station and do what she must to escape the murderers behind her. She had discovered their headquarters and they could not allow her to live. The information she had retrieved would expose every shape shifted human in Britain and France...and where the Friskmen came from.

That would be the most powerful and startling news of all.

That is why as she ran; she knew that she could expect no mercy. They sometimes tried to turn citizens willingly to their side with bribes. And it worked. Sometimes.

But they knew she was above such. They would have no mercy in their hearts...if they even had one! No mercy for her. She would die. And terribly.

Gasping for breath, she stopped.

The power station stood like a work of art at the edge of the Thames, drawing its power from the tidal surges that turned the underwater blades that fed power to the city.

The doors were wide open.

She felt her heart lurch in fear. They were there too! Her plan had been anticipated.

She shook off her paranoia. How could they have known unless...unless.

She felt violated. An Enforcer had been turned or replaced.

The doors to the power station should not have been wide open. Or open at all for that matter of fact.

Good fortune or trap?

She did not have time to parse it any further. She could hear the pounding of the Friskmen's boots on the boardwalk as they neared.

She did not even take the time to see how close they were. She would either succeed or die trying!

She dashed through the huge double doors, ran through the well-lit lobby, at once darted towards the Doors chamber, which was led to by a long corridor of piercing white marble floors and highly burnished wooden walls. Plain and utilitarian in appearance.

The door to the most powerful machine in their world was a good fifty yards ahead of her.

Ever since the Goddess of Gears had vanished for some strange reason from the Gear Worlds, most of the Door's machines had been destroyed to stop any further incursions into their world.

But this one had been kept open. Sealed by a severe form of magic that could only be broken by the man who had created it: Harry Houdini.

An old man with pure white hair, but a kindly face. He was a genius in magic and science. Without his input the Enforcers would not have lasted a day fighting the Friskmen.

She heard the pounding of heavy feet behind her and increased her pace. She had to pass several side corridors. Tense, but not daring to slow down, she continued her dash for the Doors machine.

She made it past the first two corridors, but at the third one, for no obvious reason she felt to duck.

She did.

A huge blade swept the air where her neck would have been. She ducked under it, and then kicked hard.

The Friskman standing there with the blade let out a cry of extreme pain. She had put her foot directly into its hatching sack, found pretty much where human privates were.

It doubled over in pain, letting out a hissing sound like a fish with a hoarse throat.

She then jammed her elbow into its right ear gill, and it collapsed to the floor. She leaped over it and continued her dash to the Doors chamber.

She saw lights shining in the chamber.

Again, should not have been so.

She did not hesitate.

If trouble came, she would deal with it. What other choice did she have? She needed to escape. To escape and return with the vital information her King and Queen needed to end the dominion of the Friskmen.

She had spent most of her life training for just this moment and she was not going to stop now. She was dead for sure if she did.

The double doors to the Doors Machine came close enough and she stiffened her arms and shoved hard, forcing her way inside.

A moment later the doors were struck. It almost knocked her down.

But she had been prepared. She had jammed the safety bar across both doors as she turned to add physical support.

She had prevented the monsters from getting to her at once. But they were strong. They would break the doors down. That was certain.

As her heart beat a million times a second, pounding so loud in her chest that she could hear it, she slowly turned her back to the doors.

She only had a few seconds to make a decision that was either life or death for her. For her kingdom!

Her eyes took in the vast bulk of the Doors Machine. The vast machine's gears were grinding away, toiling to move one after the other, all interconnected in both mechanical and magical ways such that the very fabric of time and space was manipulated.

It made so many kinds of sounds at the same time, she almost felt like she was at a symphony. But only for a moment.

The harsh reality struck her again.

The doors behind her made cracking sounds.

Time was up.

She searched frantically for the portal that would allow her to escape this world. She had never seen an active one and the only reason she recognized it now was because two Friskmen stepped into view in front of it, causing the air to waver behind them.

The portal!

"Drats!" She cursed.

Then she plucked the two halos attached to her belt and hefted them as she ran for the doorway.

She let out a scream so harsh and shrill that the Friskmen clasped their webbed hands over their ears to try and block the sound.

This was exactly what she needed for them to do as she leaped into the air and passing through them, still screaming, sliced their throats open from left to right and right to left and then landed inside the pulsing portal.

They collapsed to the floor behind her as she vanished in a in a pulse of blinding light.

Fraught with Nerve

One door opens
        Another closes
The depth of our choices
No one knows
But there go I
Or you
To the Sheltered Place
Where it keeps its abode
In cotton and lace.
—John Watson

Tingles and shocks ran up and down her spine as she landed hard on the balls of her feet in a dark alley.

It took her a moment to orientate herself. Her eyes were still seeing multiple flashes of light from the transition to this world and now she stood in the middle of some dark and dank place with the smell of the sea strongly pervading it.

Where was she?

The smell was familiar, but different.

She looked down. It took a few scattered moments, but then her eyes finally adjusted to the darkness she had landed within.

Cobblestones. Familiar.

But where was she?

Then she saw the Tower of Big Ben peeking above the rooftops as she gazed from the alleyway.

She smiled.

It was the right place.

But was it the right time? The right world? What if the Friskmen had invaded here as well and had plotted for her to come here so they could trap her.

Nervously, she thrust herself hurriedly out of the dark alley, again startled by the bright Tesla lights hanging from the lamppost to her right.

Once her eyes adjusted again, she noted a man dressed in a Victorian jacket, wearing a starched white shirt, and using a golden tipped cane to step along, looked both ways, and then crossed the road and headed towards her.

She stiffened.

Trap?

He got closer. His face clouded by shadows did not allow her to see his eyes clearly.

His free hand lifted.

She tensed, ready to protect herself.

Then his face was creased by a smile. "Good evening, madam."

"Could you help me?" She asked, some of her fear and tension lightening.

His smile vanished. He gave her a hard look, then said, "I'm sorry, dear Angel, but I do not require your services."

He eyed her more closely, noting her perfect posture, toned muscles and well bosomed chest. "Perhaps another time..."

She stopped his next words with a gesture.

He arched an eyebrow.

"I just want to know what time period I'm in?" She asked.

He gave her a second and even harder look, backing up slightly as if she were mad, but being a gentleman, he did not try to shoo her away.

"Queen Mary of Scots rules," he replied.

She smiled. "Good, it's the right time then."

He gave her a questioning look.

"Right time for what?"

She raised her right finger and pointed it at him. "Please, I need funds. I'll do anything to have them. Anything!"

He laughed. First, lightly, but when he saw she meant it. He roared with laughter.

"What can you, a mere lass, do or possibly do to make me want to do that?"

She scowled at him.

"Lots when we're desperate."

She felt anger growing in her. She was an Enforcer. Citizens were supposed to show respect.

His face grew solemn a moment, and then he roared with laughter again.

He stopped.

"You're serious or quite mad."

She gave him a grim look.

"My world. Your world. All words are in danger if you do not help me."

He gazed into her eyes.

"You are serious."

"I am."

"Why my money?"

"Because of whom I am. That is why. It is expected of you."

Then he backed up.

"You are either stark raving mad, madam, or you are from another world."

She sighed and looked down at her feet. She reconsidered her approach. Just because he was a man was no reason to take advantage of him. Maybe he had suffered brain damage and didn't remember the rules of law.

She looked up again. "I am sorry. I misspoke. Please, help me!"

He smiled.

"That's more like it, lass."

He was about to say more when he gasped, his eyes going to something behind her that was so large its shadow reached from the alley to overshadow him.

Crime Scene

Harry, Conan, and Challenger came running up to the alleyway, just as the same gentlemen we learned of earlier was brought forth on a stretcher. His eyes looked off into forever.

Constable Evans recognized his friends and came to greet them from the alley. "Poor chap. Died of a heart attack; I imagine."

Conan went to the stretcher as it was being loaded into the back of a siren and checked the corpse over closely. "He has all the appearances of someone struck by lightning."

Constable Evans rushed over.

"Lightning? But that is impossible; there have been no storms or electrical activity for days now."

Conan gave him a stubborn look.

"Alright, alright," Constable Evans quickly said, trying to defuse Conan's temper. "Then how did he die of an electrical shock?"

Challenger eyed the stiff posture of the man. "Every muscle in his body has contracted. He has not been dead that long, has he Conan?"

Conan bent closer to the man inside the siren and put a finger to his neck. "Body temperature indicates no more than two hours."

Harry noticed something in the man's right hand and gently pried it free, unseen by the others as he spoke. He frowned, "I've seen something like this before."

Everyone turned to look at him.

Harry turned about so they could see his face.

"Where?" Constable Evans asked.

"Germany. Doctor Frankenstein," Conan replied.

"But he's in prison now, or dead from what I've heard," Challenger pointed out.

"The man has found no jail he doesn't love," Harry said.

Constable Evans looked at him. "What does that mean?"

"That he's not likely to still be in jail if he ever was in one, and he could be anywhere," Harry remarked a bit sourly.

"Why so bitter, Harry?" Challenger demanded.

"Because the man is a lunatic. He once kidnapped Mina to use for body parts for the bride to his monster."

"That is insane. I thought he only used dead body parts," Conan hissed.

"Oh, usually, but he was especially mad at me," Harry replied, his eyebrows furrowed in thought.

"How so?"

"I blew up his castle," Harry replied, then turned about and headed for their taxi, which was waiting for them.

"Come gentlemen," he urged over his shoulder. "I think we should include someone else in this particular investigation."

"Why?" Challenger demanded, disappointed where this was going.

Harry turned about and held up a piece of cloth with gears sewn into it

Conan gasped.

Challenger's eyes narrowed. "Where did you find that?"

"Clutched in the man's right hand," Harry replied.

"And..." He pointed to a pair of footprints too small to be the man's, but also in the alley, but heading the opposite direction.

"And..." He pointed to a glistening trail of slime that rose from the cobblestones and climbed the nearest wall and over the edge of the roof.

"Dear me!" Conan uttered.

Challenger's face grew grim.

221B Baker Street

"This makes no sense," Challenger complained as Conan made a move on the chessboard between him and Challenger.

"Makes absolute sense," Conan responded, his eyes never leaving Challenger's right hand which grasped his king to move it.

"But how can something leave a woman's footprint, shock a man to death and climb a wall and leave a slime trail behind it?"

Holmes came up the stairs into the room with Watson, helping Ms. Hudson bring dinner to the boys. "That would be because you're assuming that all events are one and the same connected," Holmes explained, setting his silver tray down on the right end of the table.

Conan and Challenger at once responded by putting away the chess game.

"Standoff," Conan said.

"Exactly!" Challenger replied, getting up to help Ms. Hudson with her large tray, which was piled with several chickens roasted in herbs and applesauce. Huge chunks of apple were diced along the sides of the chicken into the bowl part of the tray.

Challenger set the tray down, dipped his forefinger into the sauce and tasted it. "To die for!" He said to Ms. Hudson.

She wagged a finger at him and said, "If you poke your finger in the food again, you will die for it!" She scolded him sternly.

Challenger gave her a mock bow, as if he had a cape and hat on, which he did not. "I bow to your majesty."

Ms. Hudson whacked him on the head with a wooden sauce spoon and he straightened up smartly.

"That hurt!"

She grinned and said, "Little boys must be treated like little boys."

And with that statement she headed for the stairs again.

Challenger gave Watson a pleading look and he shrugged, gave his friend a big grin and followed Ms. Hudson from the sitting room. "Glad it wasn't my own head for once," Watson said as he exited.

Holmes began setting plates on the table from the pantry behind it and smiled. "Face it, Challenger; you have been bested by the better sex."

"I suppose. But it hurts all the same," Challenger complained, rubbing his skull.

Conan laughed. "What a baby!"

Challenger growled at Conan but did not reply. Instead, he helped Holmes set out napkins and utensils.

"Still, Holmes, it is worrisome."

"I agree," Holmes replied. "I agree. Ms. Hudson is not usually so hot headed."

"Not that!" Challenger protested. "I'm talking about what happened."

"I agree."

Challenger looked at Holmes. "You say that with certainty."

Watson returned with coffee and tea on a tray and Ms. Hudson with vegetables and salad on another.

"That's because..." Watson yawned. "...That's because after you told us about the incident last night, we went out to take a look ourselves."

"With Constable Evans?"

"No, the young man had a date."

Challenger and Conan exchanged winks.

Holmes laughed. "Do not worry, Challenger, he has a good head on his shoulders. There is no rush to get him into the detective business. Let him enjoy his youth for a time first."

Challenger and Conan sat down and began taking food onto their plates.

Watson and Holmes did the same.

Ms. Hudson sat next to Watson and began pouring coffee. Watson nodded thanks when she filled his cup. She handed the pot to Conan, who filled his cup and Challenger's.

"I wonder where Harry is." Challenger finally said, the question having been boiling in his thoughts the whole time he had found out the man had not been expected either.

Holmes eyed Challenger.

"Harry has other plans."

Challenger gave Holmes a questioning look and Holmes explained.

Damsel in Distress

"HELP!"

Harry, who had been prowling the boardwalk for hours, raised his right fist just in case.

"HELP!" The call came again.

Female.

Harry orientated himself to the North and ran, his right fist bursting into flames. He frowned as he ran because he had not set it on fire. Which meant...?

Friskmen Attack

The Enforcer leaped into the air, kicking with all her might into the chest of the giant Friskman attacking her. But for some reason her foot did not land solidly, and she found herself tumbling to the old wood, grimy with sea salt and mold.

She struck hard; the air knocked out of her. She swiftly twisted over on her back and kicked at the webbed hands extending claws to rake her body.

The hands flew away from her, and she did a body flip and rolled between his wide legs and to the other side.

She jumped up and delivered a hammer blow to the soft spot on his head as she leaped. It struck hard, but only glanced off. Her hand, on the other hand, hurt like hell as she dropped to the boardwalk.

"Drats!" She cursed.

Then she felt something behind her.

She turned around.

It was a second Friskman.

They had followed her here.

She had hoped they would not do that. But hope is a fish without bait. It soon flies away when it is not caught in a net of well-designed logic.

She stepped away from both, but found her back to an old warehouse wall, with nowhere to go. There was no escaping right or left. They were blocking her path.

She reached for her halos to defend herself. Then she gasped in horror. They were gone.

She looked quickly at her waist belt. The loops holding the halos had been cut.

She looked up again.

The Friskman that had attacked her gave her a knowing smile. Even though the fish men were mostly expressionless, she had learned to read them regardless. Her life and those she served depended on it. The slimy thing was amused.

Then it made a sound she knew all too well. Because the last time she had heard it, her best friend had been murdered by the bastards.

She did the only thing that she could under the circumstances. She screamed.

Not once.

But twice.

She never got a third.

The Friskmen closed in on her and one clamped a slimy, webbed hand over her mouth.

"Now you die!" It slobbered from its thick fish lips in a language that few could understand.

She could.

But at that moment her language abilities and her history of how she had gotten them did not matter as it was about to end. Painfully and over a prolonged period. The fish men were cruel and used their physical strength to torture their captives into submission and then ate them.

She shuddered.

The Friskman gave her a look that said everything as its forked tongue slithered out and licked its bulbous lips.

"You will taste good!"

She felt tears coming to her eyes and tried to hide them. But too late. The Friskman about to slice her with his webbed hand claws smiled. He wanted to prolong her pain. Emotional pain was food to these evil bastards.

Satisfied it would get no more from her, it swept its hand up and back for the slash that would tear into her chest, probably cutting off one of her breasts. It was their favorite form of torture for females. And the first part they ate.

As he swept his deadly hand down, she tried to kick at him, but the other Friskman kept his legs blocking hers. She was going to die.

Horribly!

221B Baker Street

Holmes smoked his pipe by the fireplace, reading a new edition of Jules Verne's novel, "Beyond Time and Space, a Time Traveler's Tale."

It fascinated him because he knew it was not a fantasy, but an actual retelling of an event that had happened to Verne and Wells but colored in some fantasy wrappings to disguise the harsher realities of their experience.

Even though modern London had been exposed too much over the last several decades, what with the rebirth of magic and the blossoming of electric power and steam power, yet its citizens remained for the most part ignorant of the larger world and the dangers that abounded.

Holmes was not one of them.

He had traveled extensively in his early years, with is traveling stopping in India, on a distant mountain in the Himalayas and a small town called Pahalgam. He had gained much wisdom from that time and his friend, the Monk, had been the center of his newfound wisdom.

Watson sat next to Ms. Hudson, eating his fifth scone, juice drizzling across his chin.

Ms. Hudson dabbed his chin with a napkin, then kissed his chin.

He laughed. She giggled.

Holmes glanced over and smiled. It was lovely to see them so happy.

Then his own thoughts began to blur that happiness because he began thinking of Destiny again. She had not returned from her homeland for months now.

He had spoken to Lord Graystone and Lady Shareen about it, and both had assured him that the woman had left on good terms and with nothing to alarm them. But he knew her better. She could be quite persuasive when she had to be. Even elusive if necessary. And tricky, just like her father had been.

He frowned.

Was the specter of Professor Moriarty rising again?

"Holmes, you alright?" Watson asked, sensing his friend's distress.

"Perfectly fine, Watson," Holmes replied, and then returned his eyes to the words on the book's page he had been reading. They remained unreadable to him.

Finally, he set the book down and rose to his feet. "I'm going for a walk."

Now Watson was doubly alarmed. He rose suddenly, alarming Ms. Hudson, who had been cuddled next to him.

"John!" She cried out.

He reached over and brushed her hair with his hand and kissed her forehead. "Sorry, Martha. Holmes needs me."

She sighed and nodded. No one could come between those two and if they tried...she did not even want to think what would happen then.

Watson hurriedly threw on his jacket and hat and slipped into his shoes and exited after Holmes.

Challenger and Conan glanced at the chess box nearby.

"Chess?"

Conan nodded.

Battle Engaged

The webbed hand with claws came to within an inch of her face and then suddenly froze.

She gasped in surprise.

The hand glowed bright blue and a line of pure blue, like frozen blue ice, held it firm so it could not budge an inch one way or the other.

She twisted loose when the other Friskman let go to see what had happened.

The blue fire vanished from the first Friskman. She looked and they looked to see where the blue fire had come from.

Standing behind them was a well-dressed man, wearing a long coat with a fancy collar and colorful tie. He looked familiar for some reason, though at that moment she was too frazzled and stressed to go further with that thought.

"You shall not harm her!" The man warned the two Friskmen.

They turned away from her, thinking the man was the greater problem at that moment.

Big mistake.

She at once launched into the air with a kick that slammed into the back of the head of the nearest Friskman.

It let out a hideous howl, surprised, but not hurt. It only fell forward a few feet and then turned about, just as the other slashed her in a fast blow to her shoulder.

She let out a cry as her flesh was torn down to the bone and blood began flooding out.

But she did not give up.

She kicked the creature in his chest that had slashed her. But it did no better than the kick in the neck had the other.

The only result was that she lost her balance on the wet boardwalk and fell.

Then the creature raised its hand to strike her in the throat for a quick kill. Again, its hand was caught in a lasso of blue fire.

"I said stop!" The man warned. "I will not warn you again!"

It howled in pain this time. Its hand began to boil, sizzle and pop like fresh fish in an oil filled frying pan. It screamed in anger and pain. The other creature rushed in to finish her off, using the distraction to its advantage. She managed to twist aside, but again was cut in the same place. She screamed in agony, her consciousness looking to flee from the pain, but managed to hold on and see what happened next.

The man launched a blast of pure blue fire which engulfed the Friskman attacking her.

It stood there immobile for a long moment as its slimy, wet flesh began to sizzle and boil and then it let out a death cry that was so loud and ear shattering that even the other Friskman halted its advance on the man.

It stood there immobilized for a moment, its eyes looking at its hand burning in blue fire and its companion toasting on the boardwalk. It chose to not fight any longer. It fled for the boardwalks edge and flung itself into the Thames.

A flash of blue light and an explosion of heated water and no more of its presence was visible.

As she tried desperately to hang onto her consciousness, she saw the man kick the fallen Friskman over on the boardwalk, where it exploded into a final burst of blue fire and began burning briskly, and its flesh popping and crackling from the heat.

The man stepped through the raging blue inferno as if immune to its heat.

He stopped before her.

"We need to get you to a doctor."

She backed up. "I don't need anyone's help, I..."

Then she collapsed.

THE MAN REACHED OUT and grabbed her to him, swinging her upwards into his arms.

"Heavy one, this girl is," Harry said with a grin and made his way along the boardwalk towards Baker Street.

Unseen by him a webbed hand clasped the edge of the boardwalk and raised the Friskman who had fled. It raised its head over the edge, saw its burning companion and then Harry walk off.

Its face contorted horribly. It let out a cry of rage.

Harry heard it but did not turn to look.

He knew the young woman in his arms was in greater danger now than the monster that had attacked her. She was bleeding to death.

He picked up his pace, grunted, then with significant effort of will and strong young muscles began to run.

221B Baker Street

"Hurry, hurry!" Watson urged.

Harry laid the young woman on the table as Holmes and Challenger hurriedly swept the chess board and its pieces off and Conan spread a clean sheet.

Ms. Hudson produced a boiling hot pot of water, which she set on a chair.

Watson gave her a reassuring smile and nodded to the towels she had set down earlier on another chair.

She took one and dropped it into the hot water.

Watson set his black bag on the table and opened it up. "She's lost a lot of blood."

Harry nodded. "I staunched it as best I could, but for some reason her body resists magic as a healing agent."

Watson gave Harry a surprised look, then plucked a bottle of alcohol from his bag and nodded to Ms. Hudson, who gave him a hand cloth. He soaked it and began cleaning the wound.

The young woman moaned, even though her eyes never opened.

Watson sighed unhappily, and then continued cleaning her wound.

"You should have brought her to a hospital, Harry."

"I didn't dare," Harry explained. "My intuition told me she was being watched closely."

"And so, you deduced it was safer to expose your friends to danger, rather than complete strangers who hadn't a chance of dealing with these mysterious creatures you fought," Holmes said.

"Exactly!" Harry agreed, and then blushed. "Well, not quite as cavalier as you make it sound, Holmes."

Holmes smiled. "Do not get me wrong, Harry. You did the right thing, but now we are exposed as well as you."

Harry glanced at his friend. "Then you don't believe this to be an isolated incident."

Holmes did not reply, which was enough to confirm what Harry had asked anyway.

Harry joined Watson at the table. "Anything I can do to help?"

"Yes," Watson said as he pulled out a medical needle and thread. "Hold her down while I sew her back together again. This is going to hurt a lot. The wound was quite deep. A lot of nerves have been exposed."

Harry nodded and put a hand on both her shoulders. "Do your worst Doc," he said.

Watson glared at him. "I most certainly will not!"

Watson let out a huff of air, and then began sewing the young woman shoulder together again. Even with his ministrations, she might not recover. But he would fight for her life to her last breath.

Scotland Yard

Holmes and Challenger faced the Inspector over his desk. The man looked beat as usual, but he was attentive to every word that Holmes spoke.

"And so, you believe that our world has been invaded again?"

"I do."

"And if you had seen the young woman, you would have known she was not from here," Challenger added.

The Inspector eyed him sternly. "Why, did she have an extra arm or leg?"

Challenger snorted angrily but said no more.

The Inspector turned his attention back to Holmes, ignoring Challenger's scowl. "And Holmes, you know this because of this woman that Watson is caring for?"

"I do. And the murder victim began my suspicions, but she has confirmed them."

Inspector Bloodstone swept a weary hand through his mop of red hair and stared at his younger version, Constable Evans, his son, a moment. "You saw the body?"

"What was left of it. It smelled like fish."

Inspector Bloodstone snorted derisively. "They always stink when they die. Humans, I mean. But never like fish."

"I do not know why; but something about the body is not right. I just do not know what," Constable Evans explained.

He eyed Holmes again who gave a slight nod of his head.

The Inspector nodded back. He brought his hands from the back of his neck, which he had been supporting his head with. "Then I suppose we should let her majesty know at once."

He eyed his son.

Constable Evans nodded and left the office of the Inspector.

Holmes rose.

Challenger did as well.

"I believe I'd like to examine the remains of the murder victim one more time, Inspector."

Morgue

Holmes and Challenger examined the remains of the dead man's body that had been discovered in the alley.

"This is the same one that I examined yesterday," Holmes said.

"Looks dead enough," Challenger remarked.

"Yes. Quite. But something is off."

"Other than the fact that it smells like fish?" Challenger added with amusement.

"Ah-ha!" Holmes cried out.

He hurriedly snatched a surgical glove from the autopsy table and then leaned over the victim's face. As he did so, he fingered the left ear, drawing his forefinger along the outside of the ear.

As he did so the skin puffed slightly.

Holmes pried at the skin, and it began to peel away. Slowly at first, but then Holmes grabbed the edge of the skin and gave it a hard pull.

Challenger gasped at the popping sound that was made and stepped back, as if the head might explode or something horrible that had been hiding inside it was about to leap forth and attack them.

"What are you doing, Holmes?" Challenger inquired.

"Peeling his face off."

Challenger gave Holmes a blank look.

Holmes ignored it and tugged at the loosened skin he could now grab with all his fingers. Another loud popping sound and some juices spattered forth all over him and Challenger and then the skin pulled free entirely from the face.

Challenger gasped again, but not at the goo now dripping down the front of his starched white shirt, but at what had been exposed of the man's face.

It was not human.

221B Baker Street

The young woman on the table made a new moaning sound. Harry took her right hand in his and held it tight as she suddenly gave a gasping sound a cry of fear.

"You're safe!" He told her.

Her eyes fluttered open and then as her vision danced in and out of blackness, filling with splotches of color, she saw someone. Except it was not Harry.

It was a Friskman.

She at once kicked at Harry, her right leg bending up and swerving so swiftly he did not have the time to dodge it.

She sent him flying cross the room.

He slammed into the door frame and staggered a moment stunned.

She swung off the table and glared at him. "You can torture me if you wish, but I will tell you nothing!"

Harry gave her a surprised look.

Conan let out a tiny squeal from beside the fireplace.

It was the first time she noticed another man in the same room.

She at once put distance between both, backing up to the window. "Don't try anything, or I'll..."

She stopped as she reached for her halos, which were not on her belt anymore.

Harry put his right hand out. It lit up a soft blue color.

"You!" She cried out, suddenly recognizing the man before her, though not his face.

"I," he replied with a smile.

She gave him a hard look. "What are you?"

"A friend," he replied.

Conan let out a small laugh.

She turned to examine him. "You look like a comedian."

Conan stood up and clenched his hands into fists. "I'll have you know I am a world-famous author and...a damned good doctor to boot!"

She tensed her muscles, dropping into a defensive posture.

"What in the hell are you doing, Madam?" Conan demanded.

Harry stepped between them hurriedly. "Please, haven't we had enough violence?"

She surveyed Harry's face more closely now that he was between her and Conan. "Friend?"

"Yes," he replied.

She nodded and straightened into her walking posture. She headed for the exit. "Then you won't stop me from leaving."

"No, I will not. But if you leave then we will never be able to help you bring those blaggarts to justice," he warned her.

She froze midstride.

She turned around and gave him a smirk. "I don't need any man's help, thank you!"

Then her eyes rolled up in her head and she tumbled towards the floor.

The Boardwalk Alley

The morning sun was blessing the Thames with glimmers of shining gold which sparkled and glowed through the dissolving fog that hovered stubbornly above its waters.

A merchant ship sounded bells and pulled from the wharf, sails unfurling as its crew prepared it for the open sea waters.

A battle cruiser, fully armed and powerful looking, sailed into view, its twin props behind it giving it the necessary push it needed against the prevailing wind.

It angled for the wharf, where Navy men waited patiently with mooring lines and a boarding ramp.

Holmes, followed by Harry and the young woman, entered the alley.

Holmes pointed to the wall, where hints of slime remained. "Here, whatever it was, climbed to the rooftop to escape."

She nodded. "It is true. It did."

She turned to face Harry. "It was one of them."

"Them?" Holmes inquired politely.

She turned to face him again. "The Friskmen."

Holmes gave Harry a questioning look.

Harry shrugged. "She doesn't talk to me anymore."

The young woman broke into laughter. "Not only can you hurl blue fire, but you actually have a sense of humor as well."

Harry half bowed, his eyes dancing with merriment.

And for the first time since he had met her, she smiled.

Holmes waited patiently for this budding friendship to blossom, and then showed two spots.

"The body of the gentleman," he pointed to one spot.

"The spot where you stood." He pointed to another.

She glanced at the position in the alleyway and nodded. "More or less."

"Less or more?" Holmes asked.

"Exactly," she said.

"But I don't see any other footprints," Holmes explained. He pointed again to the two sets, which had been painted over for further investigation.

"You would not. They do not leave them."

"And why not?"

"Because they don't have feet," she explained.

Harry and Holmes exchanged looks.

"They have fins," she said further.

Holmes arched an eyebrow. "Interesting. Then not only are these creatures not human, but they are Pisces as well."

"What is Pisces?" She demanded.

"Fish," Holmes replied.

"Oh. Yes."

Holmes gave her a nod. "Don't you think it's time for you to explain a bit more?"

She sighed.

Harry spoke up. "Look, if you feel too traumatized."

She gave him a grateful look and an even closer look. She had not noticed how very; very handsome he was the last time. Her heart fluttered for a moment."

"No, I'm fine, except that my bloody shoulder hurts like hell!"

Both Holmes and Harry flinched from the vehemence of her sweating.

She smiled. "You two are not like the men I'm used to."

Holmes smiled. "I imagine not, since you're not from our world."

She gave him a startled look.

Holmes explained himself. "I took it upon myself to have some of your blood tested by Professor Langston, a very good friend of ours."

"And?"

"You have three kinds of blood cells. We only have two... red and white."

"Ah," she said. "I guess that would be a dead giveaway, wouldn't it?"

Harry used that moment to interject. "And we still don't have a name to go with the examination."

She gave him a shy look. "What's in a name anyway?"

He did a bold thing. He took her right hand and kissed it lightly.

She gave him another sharp, appraising look, stunned by his gesture.

He let go and smiled into her face. "It would please me greatly to give a name to such a lovely face."

She smiled back.

And for the first time, Harry felt a flutter as well. He quickly squelched it.

Mina!

Count Dracula would not smile upon a dalliance at this point in his life when he was supposed to be getting married to his daughter, even if...

And he let that thought dangle...if?

"Radiance," she replied.

"Radiance," she repeated.

"Tell us more about your...ummm... Friskmen, Miss..."

"Radiance. That is my only name," she told him.

Holmes arched an eyebrow. "When we have time, I'd like to know the story behind that."

She turned to look at Harry. "Someday, I'll tell you," she said to Harry, ignoring Holmes.

Holmes smiled. It just affirmed what he had suspected all along. The young woman was drawn quite strongly to Harry for some reason. A reason he intended to find out when time allowed for such.

Harry again felt a flutter in his heart.

"Damn!" 'He muttered, despite himself.

She gave him a startled look.

Harry at once apologized. "I'm sorry, I was just realizing something."

Homes turned to Harry.

"What?"

"The creature returned to the Thames after the battle."

Holmes nodded. "So, it must have water after a time. Which means...?"

"If we set the proper trap..." Harry added.

"It wouldn't get away!" He and Holmes said at the same time.

Radiance gave both men a look as if they had gone mad when they burst into laughter.

A Well Laid Mouse Trap for a Fish

Radiance shivered at the edge of the alleyway, pulling the shawl that Ms. Hudson had given to her for warmth tighter about her neck and shoulders. That made her grunt in pain. The cut was still quite painful, even with the exceptional care that Watson had given her.

She covertly glanced upwards and saw Constable Evans on one rooftop along with Challenger and Conan. The other rooftop had Holmes and Watson.

She knew that Harry was deeper in the alley, hidden behind a large dumpster, cloaked in a spell for extra security.

He was a curious man that Harry, she mused. Strong, handsome, and virile, yet as gentle as a child and as warm as a fresh rising sun. It made her shiver again, but this time with delight.

But this other side of him. The magical. That was worrisome. On her world most magic was not so kind as his was. Did he have a dark side to him as well?

She wanted to get to know him better. God knew she did, but she sensed there was something about him she did not know. She had sensed the spark in him that had flown between them, but he had pulled back. Why?

No time to think about that now.

She leaned against the wall by the alley exit and sighed. Life was never simple. Not these days.

Not since she would...

She cut off that train of thought as well. It led to nothing but pain and sorrow and a profound sense of loss she had taken years to bury deeply in her heart and mind. Now was not the time for the unburying of it. Her anger would flare again. Her rage. Her hatred. She could not allow that. These were good people. And she had brought evil with her.

She owed them this much at least. To help stop what might be spreading to their world as well now.

The Thames was busy with traffic this evening. Merchant ships docking. Military cruisers lying in for the night, their Navy personnel filing off to find company for the evening or a drink.

She smiled. This world was not so different from her last.

Not her own. Her last.

And again, she had to thrust the pain that had gathered so long about her heart and push it away. She sighed again. More deeply.

Then she felt something stirring.

Not at the edge of the dock. But further back, behind her, in the alleyway.

She did not know why, but somehow, she could always tell where the Friskmen were. That was why they.... rather she...had chosen this spot to spring their trap.

But now she was not so sure it had been a clever idea after all, as it seems someone was already in the trap, and they hadn't known.

Harry! A panicked thought flew through her mind.

She flung herself about, reaching for a halo.

Drats! She cursed inwardly.

She really missed her weapons.

She would have to make some new ones if time allowed. If she were still alive to do so after this night.

And as she saw the Friskmen come marching towards her from the depths of the alley...not one, not two or three, but at least a dozen...she was not so sure anymore that she would survive the evening.

The Trap Sprung

Suddenly, the dumpster that Harry had been hiding behind came barreling through the air. Straight at her. She barely had time to hit the cobblestones and roll away from the falling dumpster as it struck the stones, sending off a huge spray of fiery sparks into the air and a thunderous sound like an explosion.

"Harry!" She cried out, at once regretting it.

Half the Friskmen then turned back to look where she had been hollering to.

Harry dropped his veil of invisibility and his right fist lit up like a blow torch.

"NOW!" Holmes hollered from above.

Huge nets weighted down by heavy lead balls dropped on the first half of the Friskmen.

The second half separated and two rushed Harry, the other four rushing for her.

She backed up and reached for the long knife that Challenger had given to her. She had fallen in love with the blade at once when he had shown it to her. He had graciously allowed her to take it from his boot, where he kept it hidden.

She had spotted it at once, having done the same herself to hide her own weapons.

Thinking now, not just of herself, but of Harry who was being shoved into a corner of the alley into a shut doorway, his magic bouncing off the Friskmen like water off a duck's feathers, she screamed.

Not in fear.

But in rage. How were they countering his magic? How?

The four charging her froze for a moment. They had not expected that.

She got to within three feet of them and leaped into the air in a jump that she even felt was quite remarkable for her. She felt light as a feather when she did so.

Did this world have different laws for her than her last world?

No time to intellectualize it, she rose over their heads and slashed swiftly right and left even as the sound of police whistles and rushing men into the alley came from behind her.

The constables looked on in surprise as she landed easily on the balls of her toes, then whipped around, watching the four Friskmen tumble to the cobblestone pavement, bleeding out from the cuts she had given them on their necks.

Holmes and Watson rushed down a fire escape, as Conan and Challenger did the same from the other side along with Constable Evans to help the constables wrap up the remaining Friskmen.

The fish men continued to struggle until Harry, instead of blasting them with blue fire this time, caused a minor windstorm to blow across their slimy, scaly bodies.

The Friskmen at once stopped struggling in the net that had captured them and went limp as they starved for oxygen. Air dried out their gills and caused them to freeze, suffocating them.

She ran up to Harry, who took her hand at once and squeezed it.

"We did it!" He exclaimed, his eyes dancing with light.

She gave him a quick kiss on the lips. "Yes, we did."

Then they both stood there stunned, looking at each other.

221B Baker Street

Harry, Conan, Challenger, and Watson sat the table chatting in low voices, while Holmes sat near the fire, reading his Jules Verne book once again.

"Holmes, a game of chess?" Challenger asked.

"Not tonight, Challenger," Holmes replied.

Harry and Watson exchanged looks.

Watson turned about. "Holmes, are you alright?"

"Quite!" Holmes replied without looking up.

Conan and Challenger exchanged looks and shook their heads.

"Something's up for certain," Conan said.

"I agree," Challenger replied. "He's never like this..."

"Unless a new case has come up," Watson declared.

He turned to Holmes again. "Are we missing something, Holmes? Are you onto a new case?"

"Not yet," Holmes replied, still not looking up.

Watson scowled. "I hate it when he shuts us out like that."

"You live with him, and he still does it with you," Harry pointed out.

"Holmes is an equal opportunity denier. He will not speak until he is ready...to anyone!" Watson complained, a slight smile on his lips as he did so. He had been down this road so many times before, with this Holmes as well as the one before him, that it did not matter anymore so much. He just sighed.

"Well, here we are," Ms. Hudson announced as she and Radiance came from the stairs into the sitting room.

Harry was the last to look, but when he heard audible gasps from his friends he turned to look as well.

Radiance stood at the doorway, a big, beautiful smile on her face. No longer wearing her enforcer outfit. She was dressed in a pure white dress with red roses on its sleeves and collar.

"I made it for a friend some time back, but she moved before I could give it to her," Ms. Hudson explained. "Look. It fits perfectly on her. She looks like a princess!"

Radiance did a tiny whirl to show the dress off. "Like it?"

Challenger let out a whistle.

Radiance laughed and turned to face him. "Thank you."

"No thank you, young lady," Challenger shot back with a grin.

Then Radiance turned to Harry, who was deathly silent. "Harry?"

"It'll suffice!" He told her, steeling himself for what she would say next.

But she did not.

Instead, she gave him a look like a child might if you broke their favorite toy. She turned to Ms. Hudson. "I do not find it insufficient in anyway, Ms. Hudson. It is beautiful."

Then she burst into tears and hurried downstairs.

Ms. Hudson gave Harry a scowl. "Harry!"

She followed Radiance.

Holmes shut his book. "Harry, don't you think it's time you faced your feelings."

Harry rose stiffly. "I have someone very near and dear to me, Mina, whom I cannot bear the thought of hurting. So no, I do not think I dare do that, thank you."

Harry put on his hat and coat and trudged from the room and down the stairs.

"Wait for it!" Challenger pointed out.

SLAM!

Challenger and Conan exchanged grins.

Watson sighed. "Drama and trauma. I feel like we have become trapped in a Shakespeare play."

Ms. Hudson leaned against him as she sat next to him. "Not all things Shakespeare are so bleak, dear John."

He smiled over at her and gave her a peck on the forehead. "No, thank God. They are not!"

"And" Holmes uttered.

Everyone in the room turned to listen what he would say.

He smiled, opened his book again and said in a very pleasing voice, "No matter what the rain brings this day, there's always another day when the sun shines."

His friends burst into laughter.

Page |

Don't miss out!

Visit the website below and you can sign up to receive emails whenever John Pirillo publishes a new book. There's no charge and no obligation.

https://books2read.com/r/B-A-EMSD-GHABC

Connecting independent readers to independent writers.

Did you love *Sherlock Holmes URBAN FANTASY MYSTERIES 3*?
Then you should read *The Baker Street Universe*[1] by John Pirillo!

"I am dying!" Conan said to the Stranger who had come to him.

"No, you are not!" Professor Challenger told him. "This is just the beginning!"

In Victorian London, a doctor is dying.

And not just any doctor...but the late, great Sir Arthur Conan Doyle!

Before he passes on, he wants to make sure his wife is taken care of...

Shown just how much he truly loves and cares for her...

And finish his last Sherlock Holmes story, which will be his masterpiece!

---

1. https://books2read.com/u/bx1k0q

2. https://books2read.com/u/bx1k0q

And in another Victorian London, existing on a parallel world in a parallel universe to ours, there are heroes, heroes who exist in a world of magic and Steampunk science.

They have other plans for Conan.

To rescue him.

From death!

A deeply moving portrayal of the late Sir Arthur Conan Doyle which digs deeply into the lore about him and connects him intimately with the very characters he's written in a new universe...one of many which parallel our own.

Conan is going to be given a choice few of us are ever given...

The choice to pass on from life or to continue living...

In another universe...

The Baker Street Universe!

Where he has the chance to be part of the Sherlock Holmes team and to make friends who are true heroes, just like the ones he has written.

And even more exciting for him is the knowledge that if he does cross over into this new universe, he will be alive during the most exciting time of history!

Every writer that ever lived.

Every character that every writer has ever written.

All will be alive and existing in this parallel universe!

An Urban Fantasy Sherlock Holmes mystery novel.

Take a heartwarming and fun ride through the minds of Sir Arthur Conan Doyle, Sherlock Holmes, Watson, and so many others you have read about, but never seen in such vivid detail.

Buy your book now.

Read more at www.johnpirillo.com.

Also by John Pirillo

Angel Hamilton
Broken Fangs

Baker Street Universe Tales
Baker Street Universe Tales
Baker Street Universe Tales 2
Baker Street Universe Tales 3
Baker Street Universe Tales 4
Baker Street Universe Tales 5
Baker Street Universe Tales Seven

Between
Prince of Between

"Classic Baker Street Universe Sherlock Holmes"
Sherlock Holme: Hyde's Night of Terror
Case of the Deadly Goddess
Case of the Abominable

Detective Judge Dee
Detective Dee Murder Most Chaste

Elektron
Elektron

Escape To Adventure
Escape to Adventure

Hollow Earth Special Forces
Hollow Earth Special Forces, Forbidden World

Holmes
Sherlock Holmes Struck
Sherlock Holmes A Dangerous Act

Mystery Knight
HellBound Mystery
Hell Bound Angel

PhaseShift

PhaseShift
PhaseShift Two: Crossover
PhaseShift: Shifting Worlds

Rocketman
Rocketman
Rocket Man, Mission Berlin
Rocketman Christmas
Rocket Man, Sky Commando
Time Wars

Sherlock Holmes
Sherlock Holmes, ICE
The Ice Man
Sherlock Holmes Fallen
Sherlock Holmes: Monster
Sherlock Holmes: Tick Tock
Sherlock Holmes Christmas Magic
Sherlock Holmes Dark Secret
Sherlock Holmes Shadow of Dorian Gray
Sherlock Holmes Vampire
Sherlock Holmes: Cursed in Stone
Sherlock Holmes Apparition
Sherlock Holmes Case of the Raging Madness
Sherlock Holmes Dark Princess
Sherlock Holmes Dark Angel
Constable Evans' Fancy
Sherlock Holmes Matter of Perception
Sherlock Holmes Tangled
Sherlock Holmes Case of the Gossamer Lady

Sherlock Holmes House of Shadows
Sherlock Holmes The Yellow Death
Sherlock Holmes Oblique
Sherlock Holmes Mystery Train Winter Collection
Sherlock Holmes A Tale Less Told
Sherlock Holmes Mystery Six
Sherlock Holmes, Rules of Darkness, Special Edition
Sherlock Holmes Shape of Justice
Sherlock Holmes Christmas Magic
Sherlock Holmes Fallen Angel
Ghostly Shadows
Sherlock Holmes: Artifact
Sherlock Holmes Bloody Hell
Sherlock Holmes Monster of the Tower
Sherlock Holmes Darkest of Nights
Sherlock Holmes Nightmare
Sherlock Holmes Poetry of Death
Sherlock Holmes, Dracula
Sherlock Holmes #3, Ice Storm

Sherlock Holmes Urban Fantasy Mysteries
SHERLOCK HOLMES, URBAN FANTASY MYSTERIES 2
Sherlock Holmes URBAN FANTASY MYSTERIES 3
Sherlock Holmes, The Dracula Files
Sherlock Holmes, Dark Clues
Sherlock Holmes, Case of the Undying Man
Sherlock Holmes, Mystery of the Sea
Sherlock Holmes, Night Watch
Sherlock Holmes, Mystery of the Path not Taken
Sherlock Holmes, the Dorian Gray Affair
The Baker Street Universe

Sherlock Holmes, The Dracula Affair
Baker Street Universe Tales 6
Spector

The Baker Street Detective
Strange Times, The Baker Street Detective, Book2
The Baker Street Detective, Hollow Man

Standalone
Sherlock Holmes Deadly Consequences
Invisibility Factor
Red Painted Souls
Between
Robin Hood
Shadow Man
The Rainbow Bridge
Cartoon, Johnnie Angel
Sherlock Holmes 221B
Sherlock Holmes Shape Shifter
Urban Fantasy Mysteries
Sherlock Holmes, Urban Fantasy Mysteries

Watch for more at www.johnpirillo.com.